Renegade Angel

Angel Academy Book 3

KATE HALL

Lost Window LLC

"Chaos is an angel
who fell in love with a demon."
Christopher Poindexter

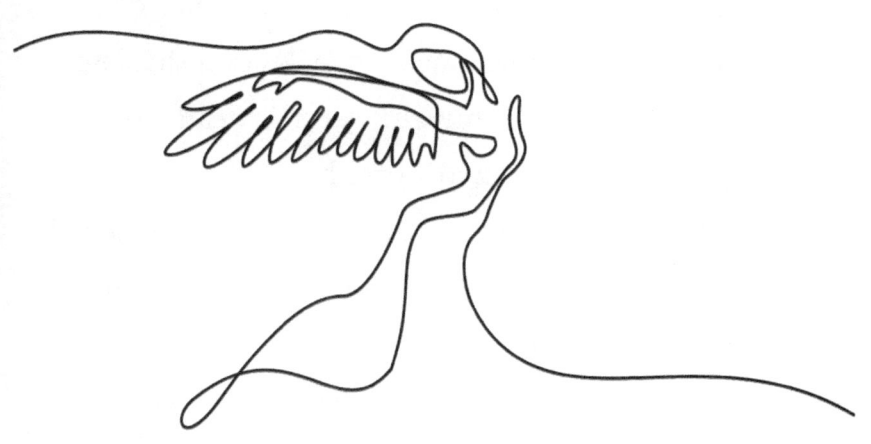

Chapter One

I am about to meet with Lilith. My leg bounces as I sit in the waiting room, eyes darting around nervously. Dad is sitting awkwardly next to me, somehow still sober even though my accident was nearly a week ago. He hasn't gone without drinking this long in years. Not since Mom died, at least.

"What time is the funeral?" I ask. Desireé's service hadn't been announced in the papers, only the fact that she died. Her mom doesn't want everyone in a hundred mile radius showing up, mainly because the only funeral home and cemetery in town can only hold a hundred or so people.

He watches my face carefully, still waiting for me to freak out, I presume. I haven't cried since he told me that Desireé, my girlfriend, is dead, and it seems like it's starting to worry him.

"Five," he says, then chews his lip. Just as he's about to open his mouth to speak, a nurse with a long beard and teal scrubs calls my name.

I stand up and rush to the door. I don't want to have an emotional conversation with my suddenly concerned father. It's not going to help anything, and, for now, I need to focus on rescuing Desireé from the angels that have taken her captive.

When I enter the exam room, I stay standing, ready to bolt through the door at any time. This is the first demon, the mother of all evil, after all.

After I've only been waiting a moment, Lilith enters the room. She looks totally normal, a medium-height woman with dark skin, a long, elegant nose, and a white lab coat. Still, I know what lurks under the surface.

At least, I thought I did. Now, I can't be so sure. If she's the first demon, the one who followed Lucifer into Hell, then why hasn't she killed me yet?

Maybe she's just toying with me.

"I think we can help each other," she says without even saying "Hello."

My hands ball up into fists, and my eyes narrow. "How do you think?" It's against every cell in my body to trust a demon, especially this demon. I try not to think about the fact that I'm in love with another demon. She's different, though.

I'm pretty sure she is, anyway.

Lilith smiles, her entire body relaxed. Of course she has nothing to worry about. Even if I were to summon my sword, there's nothing I could do to fight a demon that's survived through a few millenia of wars and tension. "I don't want Desireé to go to Hell. I like her. She's good at what she does. She's more bloodthirsty than a lot of the demons in our ranks."

This only stands to remind me that Marcus, another demon, once described Desireé as ruthless. That can't be right. Not my Desireé, anyway. "You don't know what you're talking about."

She laughs, her tone airy and light, nothing like what I would expect of a demon. "I don't want to be a part of yet another war, Avery. And, if you haven't noticed, you're kind of starting one."

This throws me, and my mouth pops open. I've been an angel for less than a year. What power would I have to start a war? "That doesn't...I can't...I'm not..."

Lilith rolls her eyes and leans against the counter, then peers directly into my own eyes. "Angels and Demons are not supposed to love each other. It shouldn't be possible. This whole debacle has the higher-ups questioning shit on both sides. And I feel like I should remind you that this sort of thing doesn't usually end up with everyone singing Kumbaya around a campfire."

I grit my teeth to keep myself from spitting out some witty retort. She could still kill me if she chooses. She says she needs my help, but surely someone else could do the job in a pinch if I were dead. Instead, I consider my words before saying, "But aren't we already in a war?"

I expect her to laugh, to roll her eyes again, anything, but instead, her eyes go dark.

"No," she says.

I stand in silence, letting her gather her thoughts.

Finally, she continues, "The last war was thousands of years ago. It was awful, too. Demons and angels slaughtered at every turn." Her eyes bore into mine, and I'm rooted to the spot. "People. They were people, and they were killing each other just because Cain decided where they should be. Friends. Lovers. Parents and their children. It didn't matter." She sighs, and a shuddering breath comes out. I didn't know that the mother of demons could sound so sad. At this moment, it's clear to me just how ancient this gorgeous woman really is. "I've been through this many times, Avery. So damn many. And I just can't do it again. I'm tired."

I wrap my arms around myself as a sudden chill takes to the room. How am I supposed to respond to that? Do I comfort her? Talk to her? Ask about it?

I frown. "I planned on saving Avery anyway, you know. You didn't have to corner me and make me terrified of every move I make."

Lilith's heartbroken exterior fades, and she tilts her head. Her eyes glimmer with amusement.

5

"I'm not here to intimidate you, Avery."

I open my mouth to point out that she's the most deadly creature I've ever met, but she holds up a finger.

"Do you really think that the Archangels don't know where you are?"

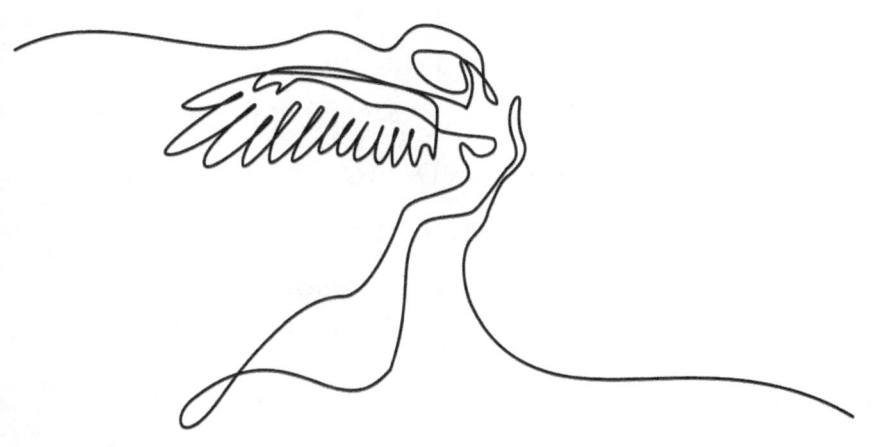

Chapter Two

I don't respond. I can't. I've felt totally alone since returning home, although Dad has been hovering over me quite a bit. Am I being watched, though? Are the Archangels just waiting for an opportunity?

Were Nicolai, Huỳnh, and Gabe caught after helping me escape? Or trying to release Desireé?

If they were, what have the angels done to them?

My hands shake, and I have to clench them into fists to keep Lilith from seeing. She can't see me as weak, although, right now, I feel anything but strong. I have to seem like it, though, or she'll dispose of me and pick someone else.

"The only reason we need you," Lilith says, not seeming to catch my distress, "is to find out where the angels are keeping Desireé. We believe that she's still alive, and you're the key to getting her out. If you bring her to us, we can protect her." She pauses, then purses her lips with obvious distaste before continuing, "We can protect you as well."

What does that even mean? Am I going to be taken to Hell? Not to be tortured, but to be…protected?

I don't really want to know what's going to happen after I save Desireé. I can only handle one thing at a time, and I'm really not handling this all that well as it is. I haven't slept, haven't stopped wondering how much longer I'll be alive.

"Why?" I ask.

She shrugs, leaning back in her chair casually. "Consider it a favor."

I shudder. The last demonic favor I'd been involved in had ended up with me cornered in an alleyway by Marcus, a demon who'd ripped up the skin at the base of my wings during a scuffle.

I don't really know that I can trust a favor from a demon.

I look out the window, studying a pair of small brown birds that flit from branch to branch. "Do I really have a choice?"

Lilith's mouth twists into one of her menacing smiles, and she sits back up. "Not really. If you don't help us, we will have no reason to protect you."

Goosebumps raise on my arms as I imagine what might happen if the Archangels find me. The demons may be a clear and present danger, but maybe I should be thankful that they're here at all.

"Fine," I say, extending my hand for a shake. She reaches to me and takes it, her hand so hot that it's like taking an iron in my grip. I grit my teeth and force myself to keep from pulling away. *Don't show weakness.*

"I'm glad we could come to an agreement," she says. "You'll be seeing us around." I nod, and she hands me a familiar device made of black crystal. It's a phone of sorts, except this one is made to contact people in different realms. I'd used a device just like this to speak with Desireé while I was in Heaven. "Call me if you need anything."

I just nod in response.

I am going to be surrounded by demons.

I have to find out how to rescue Desireé from the Angels. The good guys. And then, I will be going to Hell.

I swallow and try to convince myself that this is fine.

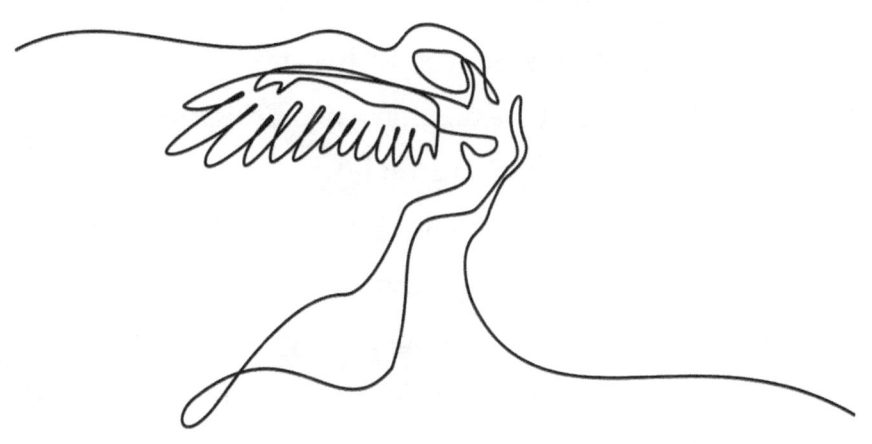

Chapter Three

It doesn't rain at Desireé's funeral. In fact, it's an unseasonably sunny day, far too cheery for the way I actually feel. She has a closed casket service, probably because her body had never been recovered from the river.

Everyone says that it's a miracle that I survived with no injuries. They have no idea that I should be dead, too, but I'm sure many of them are thinking it. Desireé had been perfect. The epitome of a good person. And now she's dead.

I stay quiet and keep my hands tied together behind my back, trying to look sad and respectful, when really, my mind is racing through different ways I might be able to find her. It shouldn't be that hard, right? I mean, I have mystical powers.

And very little training on how to use them.

As the sermon draws to a close, I take in a deep breath. I'm supposed to give a speech about Desireé, something to reassure everyone, to quell their anger at my survival. The only problem is, almost everyone in town despises me. I can't blame them, of course. I'd done some awful things while I was alive, including getting a teacher fired for an affair I'd completely made up in order to extort money out of him.

I can hardly believe that Cain agreed to Desireé's terms to send me to Heaven, but, on the other hand, she'd let Nicolai in, and he'd been a Russian gangster who killed people.

I wasn't the worst Angel in Heaven, but still.

After Desiree's mom stumbles her way through a speech, her eyes glazed with sadness and probably several forms of medication, it's my turn. I go up to the podium, keeping my eyes away from the empty casket. Did they put some of her clothes in there or something? What's the point of a funeral with no body? *She isn't gone,* I remind myself. *She's somewhere else. And I'm going to bring her back.*

When I look out into the crowd, though, I see nothing but sadness and hatred. She may be alive to me, but to everyone here, she's dead, and I'm the reason she died.

"Desireé is…" I pause. "Was. She was the love of my life. And I would do anything to have her with me again." My throat closes up as I wonder if saving her is something I can actually accomplish. "She was the best person I knew. The best person any of us knew." Then, I say something I've been thinking for months, since I first found her infiltrating Heaven. Something that, at the very least, these angry and sad people will agree with. "She didn't deserve what happened to her."

Something wet splashes on my hand, and I look up to find out if it has somehow begun to rain, but the sky is as clear as it's been all day. I blink, and a fat tear rolls down my cheek.

"I'm sorry," I croak, then run from the stand. I don't make eye contact with her parents, don't look at the casket. I can wait in the car until Dad's ready to leave. There's no way I can spend a moment longer at this funeral, though. It's just too much.

We're parked up the road, past a huge line of cars. When I get there, though, there's a tall boy with brown hair leaning against Dad's old pickup. He looks so unassuming on Earth, just a normal teenage boy, but I know what lurks beneath the surface.

"What's up, Avery Two?" Marcus, my least favorite demon, asks.

I grit my teeth.

"Hello, Marcus," I say, forcing myself to be civil. Marcus may have done a favor for Desireé by giving me the phone back at Theaa Academy, but he's definitely no ally of mine.

A lazy smile crawls across his face, and I grimace.

"I guess Lilith told you we'd be hanging out, right?"

No, she absolutely had *not* mentioned Marcus. She may be the mother of demons, but I definitely would have protested *him* being here.

"Of course," I say nonchalantly. My relaxed demeanor seems to throw him off, just enough that his eyes flicker with the slightest bit of confusion. "I look forward to having a personal bodyguard that can't beat me in a fight."

He snarls and starts to lunge toward me, but his eyes flick somewhere behind me. I don't take the bait, don't turn around. He will not trick me into turning my back to him, not for a moment. Not after what his demonic talons did to my wings.

"Well," he says, "that's debatable."

I shrug. "Listen, if you need something, you can text me. I need to head out, though, and you're in my way." I take the Hell phone out of my pocket, the black crystal seeming to suck in all the daylight around it like it's starving.

He smirks and moves out of the way, and I open the pickup truck door, climbing in.

"See you at school tomorrow," he says.

I close the door, blocking him out. He gives me one last asshole smirk, then disappears.

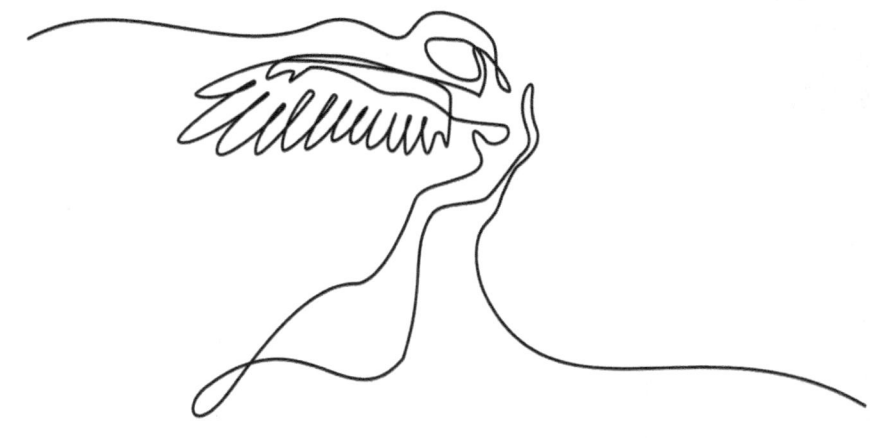

Chapter Four

On the way home, I remain perfectly silent. Dad doesn't try to talk to me, but I catch him looking at me more than a few times. When we arrive at the house, a single-wide mobile home which is in severe disrepair, I sigh. There's a small porch leading to the front door, and the wood is a bit too mushy for comfort. The car Dad bought with my wreck's insurance money sits in the overgrown gravel drive, a tan Nissan that's probably older than the Archangels themselves, give or take a few years.

I walk past a separate rusted car that's being

eaten by the plant life slowly but surely. When I enter the house, I have to hold my breath. It's a lot cleaner than when I was actually alive. Dad must have done something about the mess while I was in the hospital, which is out of character for him. Still, the ancient house smells musty and dank, like it's been sitting in a humid swamp for years. I don't really want to start coughing, so I just don't breathe when I'm in here. I save that for the fresh outdoor air.

The floor of the kitchen is bare particle board, and I glance at a part of the corner that seems to be dry-rotting away. The vinyl floor had been ripped up years ago, back when Dad first decided to fix the place up. He gave up pretty quickly.

"Do you want dinner?" Dad asks, but I shake my head.

"I think I'm just gonna turn in early," I say. I won't sleep, though. I haven't slept a wink since I arrived back on Earth, but it's not as though I need to.

He nods, his face a half frown. "Okay. Remember you have school tomorrow."

"Right," I say, my voice filled with distaste.

He pauses, then says, "Are you sure you're okay to drive tomorrow?"

His wariness is understandable. The last time I drove a car, in his mind, was when I drove over the side of a cliff into the river. He hadn't protested buying me another vehicle, though, so he can't be completely against the thought of me behind the wheel again. "Yeah, I'm good. I promise."

He doesn't seem so sure, but he doesn't argue. I turn my back to him and go to my room, lying on my bed. I take out the black phone, turning it over and over in my hands. I don't have a way to call anyone except for Lilith, as her name is engraved in the demonic sigil language on the back. Lying here reminds me of earlier in the term, which, really, wasn't so long ago. I would sit in my little secret cubby and call Desireé. Even though she was in Hell because of me, she always seemed happy to talk to me. I will forever be grateful for her love, and I have to pay her back by making sure the angels don't harm her.

An idea begins to form in my head, although I

have no idea how I'm going to pull it off.

Still, I have to try.

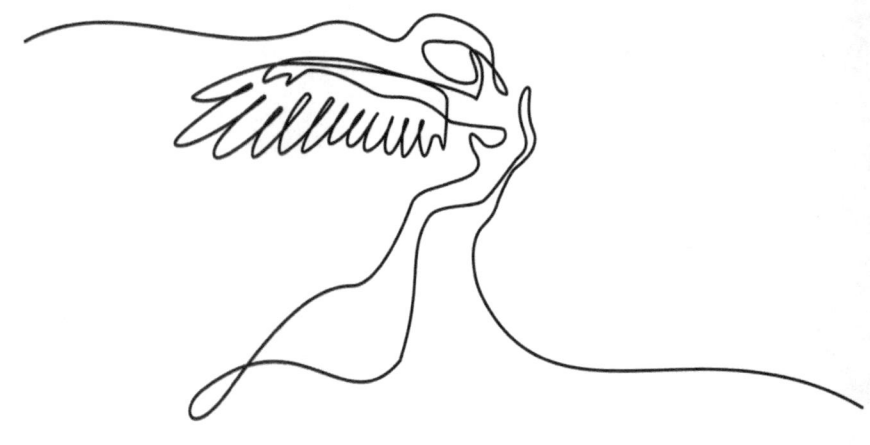

Chapter Five

School is absolutely jarring. I've spent nearly a year in an academy filled with angels, being taught how to fight and kill demons as well as the history of eternal beings. Now, though, I'm expected to attend Math class?

I sigh with frustration as I pull into the school's lot in the ancient Nissan that's not nearly as fancy as the Audi I'd been driving on my Earth missions with Gabriel. Lilith had called me overnight, ordering me to just sit tight, which has me anxious, and I can't help but pull my itchy sweatshirt a little tighter around my body. I hate human clothes.

They're far too rough against my sensitive angelic skin, and I just wish I could have my luxurious silky uniform made of heavenly materials back.

I guess I'll just have to deal with jeans and a sweatshirt instead.

I ignore the stares of everyone when I walk into the building. I hadn't been well-liked before the accident, and Desireé had been my only friend on Earth. She'd been everything to me, and now she's dead. Gone forever, at least as far as these people are concerned. Now, though, there's straight hostility in their glares. I won't be surprised if someone tries to start shit with me before the end of the day.

My first class is multimedia, which means I can finally get to a computer. My phone had been lost in the accident, so I've had absolutely no access to the internet since I came back to Earth. Since I can't go to an ethereal library containing all the books in the universe, the school's slow connection will have to do.

Luckily, I'm at the back of the room in a corner. I angle the screen just a little so that the boy two seats away doesn't see, and I open Google.

How to Summon an Angel.

Most of the answers involve prayer, and there are tons of articles and books about guardian angels. Not what I'm looking for at all. I keep scrolling, and it isn't until the eighth page that I find something even a little promising.

The link is for a dingy website with red text over a black background. Mid-2000s occult stuff. This should work. At the very least, the spell is written in Enochian, the language of angels. I print it out, and the teacher gives me the stink-eye but doesn't say anything about my disruption after he reads the first line of my article. His anger turns to pity, and he holds out the too-thick stack of paper. "Thanks," I mumble, scurrying back to my seat.

The pity that comes with a dead girlfriend can be used to my advantage, as it turns out. If I do anything weird having to do with angels, Heaven, or Hell, people will just assume I'm mourning in my own way. It's sort of true. They just don't know for sure that it's all real. That I've been to Heaven.

That I'm still an angel, and I'm trying my hardest to bring Desireé back.

I read over the article and ignore the teacher's lecture. He doesn't even tell me to pay attention, which is fine by me. I have better things to do than invest in school when Desireé's immortal soul is on the line.

Nobody tries to mess with me, which is a bit of a shock. It hadn't been easy for Desireé and I, the only lesbian couple in our tiny school, and now that she's gone, I've been expecting the other students to target me like they did before she and I became a couple.

At lunch, I sit at my usual empty table at the back of the cafeteria. A moment later, though, two others join me.

Marcus I recognize instantly, and I frown but don't speak. I will not give in to his taunting. The girl, though, is a tall blonde that I don't know. Still, there's something in her features that gnaws at my subconscious. Have I had a class with her before? It wouldn't surprise me if Marcus somehow roped a human into spending time with him.

"What's your name?" I ask, not even trying to

sound kind.

Her eyes narrow.

"Nadia."

All her familiar features click into place. The slope of her nose, the set of her chin, the pale eyes. Of course. She looks familiar because she looks so much like her little brother. I gape, and whisper, "You're Nicolai's sister."

The brother that got her killed. The one whose place she took when Cain led them to the afterlife.

Here eyes widen, and the breath comes out of her in a rush. "How do you know Nicolai?"

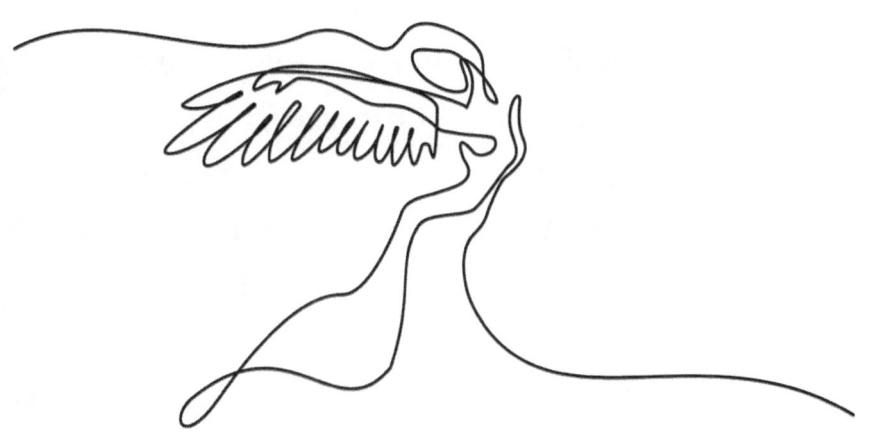

Chapter Six

It's the middle of the night when I'm finally able to try the printed spell. I skip the part about lighting candles and drawing a sigil on the ground. I've never seen a single angel use sigils to perform a spell. They're mainly used to communicate. Maybe it's a human thing.

I repeat it three times, my tongue turning expertly over the Enochian words that have become like a song to me. Even though I'm the one speaking it, it's comforting to hear the mystical language of angels. Almost like being back at Theaa Academy.

Almost instantly, a bright, Heavenly light appears in my room, and I have to cover my eyes. I'm not used to the brightness of Angels anymore, just the plain normalcy of Earthen lighting.

The light fades quickly, and a young man is standing in my bedroom, his soft blonde hair and tall stature instantly familiar and comforting. I run to Nicolai and wrap my arms around him, and he cusses under his breath when my body slams into him.

"Hi, Avery," he says just a little too loudly. I shush him as quickly as I can, then strain my ears to listen, but it doesn't sound like Dad heard. At the very least, he's not coming to investigate.

When I pull away, Nicolai looks around, a slow smile creeping onto his face. "This is your room," he says. His features are open and boyish, and he has the pale blonde hair of his Earth form instead of his snow-white Heavenly hair.

I nod. "Yup. Anyway, more importantly, we need to talk about Desireé."

He sighs and nods. "We're trying," he says. "It's hard, though. Gabriel is suspicious of everyone since what happened to you."

I nod. "I know, I know. But you sent me back to the point of my death. I thought you would do the same with Desireé."

He doesn't seem to have a response to that, so he goes to the bed and sits.

"Well?" I ask after a too-long silence.

He shakes his head. "I don't know. You know time is different in Heaven. And I sent you back to the moment of your death because I figured it would be safest. That...sounds like what I would do with Desireé, too."

"Well, we'll have to do something. Because if you do what you're doing now, I don't think you're going to save her."

He nods, closes his eyes, takes a breath, and then looks at me.

"Alright. What are we going to do?"

I shake my head. "I have no idea, but there is someone who might be able to help us."

He quirks his head, but he doesn't ask. My heart races in my chest, pounding like it's trying to escape. I swallow to get rid of the lump forming in my throat.

"Well?" he asks when I remain silent for far too long.

I can't keep eye contact with him for this, so I look at the ground. "Your sister." I let out a shaky breath. "Nadia is here. On Earth. At my school."

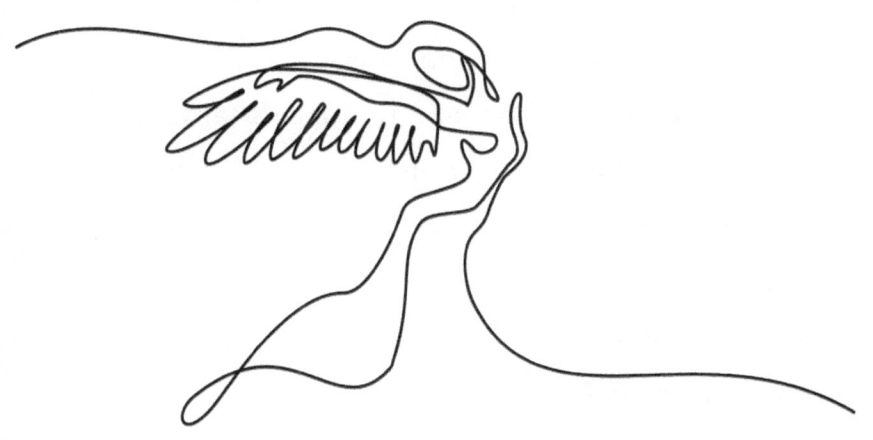

Chapter Seven

Nicolai looks like he's just seen a ghost.

I mean, I guess I sort of just told him that his dead sister is alive. Ish.

"How can you be sure?" he says, his voice breathy and strained. His eyes are suddenly hollow and glazed.

"I saw her," I say. "She's one of the demons they put in charge of watching me."

"They?"

Right. I haven't told him about the situation with Lilith. I explain it as quickly and succinctly as possible, but he doesn't appear to really be listening. Probably because of the life-changing revelation I just dropped on him.

"Nicolai?" I ask when I'm done. It takes him a moment to blink and look at me, and when he does, his features are shell-shocked. I frown. "Please say something."

He opens his mouth, then closes it, then opens it again. "How is she?"

I sigh. "I don't really know. I mean, it's hard to tell."

He nods. "Okay." Changing gears, he says, "Well, what's the plan?"

It's my turn to be unsure. Through all this, I haven't really come up with anything to do. The plan had been to summon Nicolai and ask him what the plan is. "I think the first step is to figure out a way for us to communicate, that way I don't have to summon you or hope you show up or something."

"Alright. I'll get a phone soon. Or Huỳnh can. Or Gabe."

I frown. "I don't want them to get involved. It's so dangerous already."

He rolls his eyes and cracks a smile, but it

doesn't quite reach his eyes. "They're already involved. Just take the damn help."

I make a frustrated sound and sit on my floor, which Dad must have actually had washed, because it doesn't smell faintly of cat pee from the previous homeowners anymore. "Fine," I finally say. "Fine."

He nods, then his smile widens. "They hooked up last week."

I gasp, and my eyes widen. "I knew it!"

He laughs, telling me all about it. How they'd been caught in one of the activity rooms by another student, how they'd been formally chastised by Gabriel and Azrael for being so inappropriate in a public space.

This conversation almost feels normal, and I almost forget about the target on my back and the ticking clock to save the love of my life.

Almost.

After chatting and gossiping for a while, the sky outside goes from black to a pale gray-blue. Somehow, it's already morning, and Nicolai has been here all night.

"I should probably go," Nicolai says, staring out the window. I lie back in my bed, which we're both now sitting on, my legs propped over his.

"Ugh," I say. "I have to go to school in an hour."

"That doesn't sound so bad," he says, removing my legs from his lap so he can stand.

I roll my eyes. "Trigonometry is that bad. I promise."

He smiles, but his eyebrows are tilted up with sadness. "Tell Nadia I said hello." After an awkward pause, he continues, "And I'm sorry."

"Okay," I say, gently placing a hand on his. I stand, and, in the small room, that means we're practically touching. I wrap my arms around him, and, after a moment, he returns the hug. "See you soon," I mumble.

"Right," he says. "If we don't get killed first."

I sigh.

"Right. That's all."

I really hope we don't get killed.

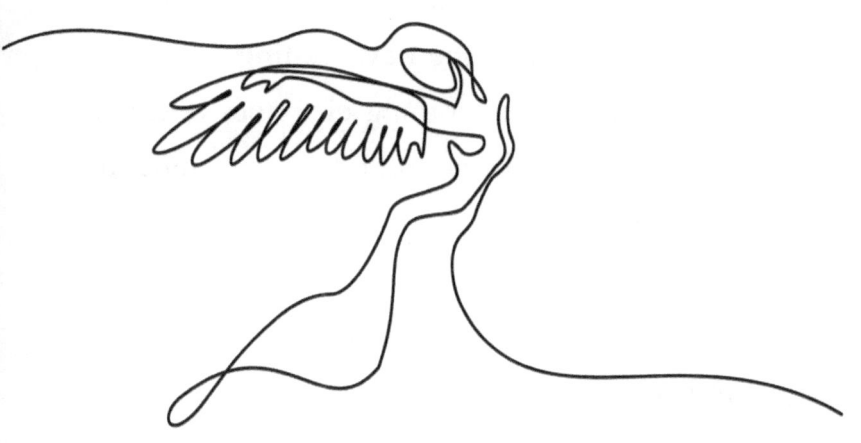

Chapter Eight

Whent I arrive at school, there's a note spray
painted on my locker.

I wish you'd died.

It's written with red spray paint, and I glance
down the hallway, but whoever wrote it is nowhere in sight. The note is already dry, so it had to
have been done a while ago. Probably yesterday.

Whatever. It won't matter soon.

I walk away from my locker and head to class,
ignoring Marcus's eyes on me as I pass him in the
hall. How many other demons are in the school? I
probably don't want to know, but I can't help but

be suspicious of every student I can't quite place.

I shamble through the day, waiting for something to happen, but nothing else does. I'm still ignored in all my classes, and I don't catch anyone staring at me.

When I walk out to my car, though, there's another note in the same red letters.

Die, bitch.

I take a deep, shuddering breath. I can deal with this. A tiny bit of bullying is nothing in comparison to the hardships coming up. My hands ball up into fists, and I have to shake them out before getting into the car. Dad had finally given me a new phone last night, and I open it to find that I have several messages.

Are you coming in to work?

I know your girlfriend died, but I need you to come in.

Text me back!!

I sort of forgot that I had a job on Earth, one that involved serving greasy burgers to people who bought them and looked down on those of us who had to make them.

I consider texting my manager back, but, knowing the mood I'm in, it will not be a pleasant response. As an angel, I should at least try to be a decent person, right?

I'm definitely not going into work, though. That's just too much.

When I get home, a small box is on my bed, shipped all the way from Kansas City.

I don't recall ordering anything online before I died, but I was in Heaven for nearly a year before I woke up in that hospital bed. I rip the package open, and inside is a piece of translucent rose quartz about the size of my hand.

I guess Nicolai or Huỳnh or Gabe got my Heaven phone, after all. With the weird way time works, any one of them could've sent it well before I summoned Nicolai to my room.

Although I'm not fluent enough in Demonic runes to call anyone other than Lilith on the black phone—which sits unused in my sweater pocket—I scrawl Huỳnh's name in Enochian on a sheet of paper and press the rose quartz device down.

Almost instantly, it glows, and an electric tingle

runs up my arm.

"Avery, thank god," Huỳnh says almost instantly. Unlike the Hell phone I'd kept secret in Heaven, Huỳnh's voice is as clear as a bell, almost like she's in the room with me.

"Huỳnh," I breathe, my friend's face flooding me with relief. Every day, I wonder, in the back of my mind, if I'd imagined everything about Heaven. Rationally, I know I didn't, but still, the doubt creeps in. Seeing my friend's face relieves that ache just enough that I can breathe again.

"I don't have a lot of time," she says. "Class starts in ten minutes." Her strawberry blonde hair is pulled up in a loose ponytail, and her tan skin practically glitters in the angelic light of Heaven. I sigh with longing as I imagine being back there, in a world where everything was perfect and magical.

Everything except the part of my life that matters most, anyway.

"I need to find Desireé," I say.

Huỳnh nods. "I know. Nicolai filled us in. We're trying. It's hard, though. The Archangels are keeping everything a secret. Nobody can get any information out of them. Not after what happened with you."

I nod. That makes sense, of course. If one angel can defect because of a demon, why not all of them? "So what's the plan?"

She looks off to the side, then back at me. "I'm not sure. I'll let you know when I have more information. I have to go." Before I can protest, she's gone.

I don't have time to be sad about it when a knock comes softly at my door.

"It's open," I say, shoving the magical phone in my pocket. I hope carrying three phones around isn't too noticeable.

Dad opens the door just a little, enough to poke his head in. "You have a friend here to see you."

I frown. I don't have any friends. Not on Earth, anyway.

"Who is it?" I ask. When he opens the door wider, Nadia is standing next to him, eyes smoldering.

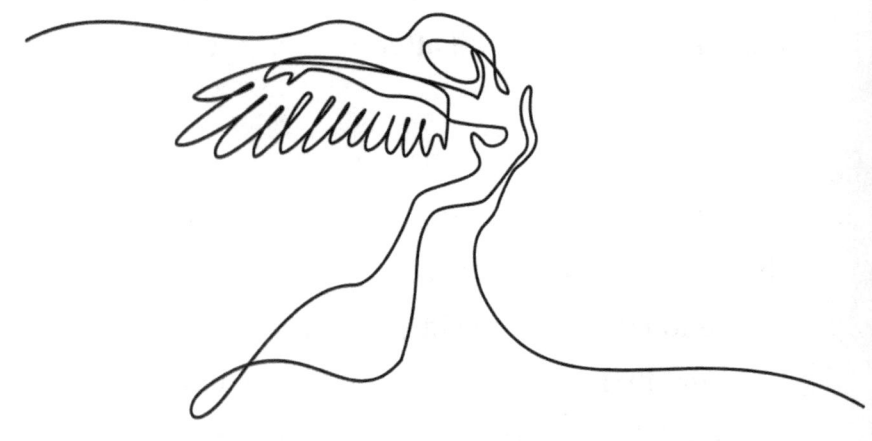

Chapter Nine

"What do you want?" I hiss after she shuts the door behind her, blocking my dad out.

She doesn't give me the same cocky smile that Marcus always seems to have, though. In fact, she's a lot quieter than him. She almost reminds me of Desireé by her subdued demeanor.

"What do you know about my brother?" she asks, her voice soft, cracking on the last word.

Oh. That's not at all what I was expecting.

"Nicolai?" I ask, but of course that's who she's talking about. Who else could she mean?

She doesn't make fun of my stumble though.

Instead, she just nods. She looks out the window, avoiding my eyes. What is she thinking right now?

"I know you two grew up in Saratov, Russia," I say carefully. She frowns but doesn't return her eyes to mine. "I know he was involved with a gang, and that's how you got your apartment."

Her face crumples, and a tear streams down. Even when Desireé was with me at Theaa Academy, I never saw her cry. Not once. This show of emotion from Nadia is a shock, and I'm not sure how I'm supposed to respond. "I didn't believe it," she says. "When Cain told me. I thought it was a lie, or that she had it wrong."

I shake my head. "No," I breathe.

Finally, her eyes return to mine. "Thank you," she says. I half expect her to turn around and leave, but she doesn't. She just stands there and watches me. After a moment, she opens her mouth like she has something to say, then rethinks it.

"He didn't want to hurt you," I say. "Everything he did was to make sure you were okay. He didn't want to hurt anybody."

She doesn't respond, just looks away. She's not

even breathing.

I sit on my bed, then pat the spot next to me.

"Sit," I say. Maybe I shouldn't be assertive with a demon I don't know, but she listens to me, joining me on the ancient comforter. I tell her about Nicolai. Not the crimes he admitted to committing before his death, but how he was in Heaven. The kindness in his eyes, the jokes, the playfulness. At some point, Nadia's head rests on my shoulder, her hair streaming down my arm. I don't protest.

I keep talking, and, eventually, she breathes again. After that, her breaths turn soft and slow, and her head becomes heavy on my shoulder. I sigh and carefully maneuver her so she's lying down, then cover her with a soft throw. If she's anything like Desireé, then she probably hasn't slept since she went to Hell. She needs this.

I scroll through the internet on my normal phone, the one Dad bought me, looking for any sort of information that could help, but I come up short. Dad doesn't check in on us. He may be a better parent than before the accident, but he doesn't seem aware that teenagers don't usually stay the night with their friends on a school night. Oh, well.

Just as the sun is rising in the morning, Nadia sits up, her blonde hair like a halo of tangles around her. I smile gently, but she doesn't respond in kind.

"I had a thought," she says. Her voice isn't groggy. Much like when I would sleep in Heaven, she simply went from being asleep to being awake. There is no in-between.

I tilt my head and lock the phone.

"Angels can sense each other on Earth, right?" Her eyes bore into mine, like this is the most important question with the most important answer in the world. I nod. "Demons can do the same."

This is news to me, although it makes a lot of sense. While demon auras are like a void of nothingness to angels, they might seem different to other demons, much like I feel when I'm around other angels.

"So, if this is true, why hasn't anyone tracked Desireé? If she's so important, I mean?"

I open my mouth to answer, then close it again.

It's that simple, isn't it?

If Desireé were on Earth, then a demon should be able to track her. Even if it were really difficult, someone like Lilith should have no problem finding her, right?

"I have to make a call," I say.

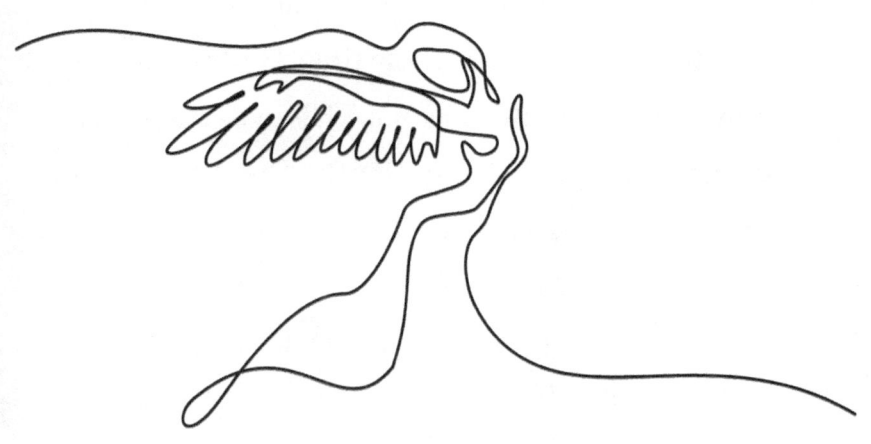

Chapter Ten

It's only a few seconds before Nicolai answers my call.

"Avery, is everything alright?" he asks after taking in my face.

"Sort of," I say. I don't give him a chance to speak, continuing, "I know where Desireé is."

He squints at the screen, then freezes. When I turn around to find out what he could be looking at, Nadia is standing behind me, no longer lying in my bed.

"Nadia," he says, his word coming out choked.

She nods. "Hello, Nic."

"I know this whole thing is important you you," I say, feeling awful the whole time, "but we have a more pressing matter, Nicolai." His eyes snap back to mine. "Desireé isn't on Earth. The Archangels must be holding her in Heaven."

His eyes widen. "Of course," he says. "They can't risk her being on Earth, not when everyone is looking for her. Not when there's a war at stake!"

I nod excitedly. "So we just have to get her out of there. And then it'll all be okay." I can't be certain of this, of course. Lilith claims that Desireé's death would trigger a war, but what if her freedom would do the same? How many beings would die and be sent to purgatory? And, sureley, we'd have to stay in hiding. We would never be able to leave Hell again, not with every angel in heaven looking for us.

"Are you sure about this?" Nicolai says. I want so badly to say yes, to be selfish so that I can have Desireé safely by my side, but I can't lie.

"No," I say. "Honestly, it could make everything a lot worse. But we have to do something. If Desireé is killed, there will definitely be a war."

He hesitates, and Nadia says, "Nicolai, we have to do this." He frowns, then finally nods.

We just have to come up with a plan.

I turn back to Nadia and utter words I never thought would come out of my mouth. "We're going to need Marcus's help to pull this off."

Nicolai goes pale. He's interacted with Marcus all of one time, which would be more than enough for anybody.

"Fuck," he says.

I sigh. "Exactly what I was thinking."

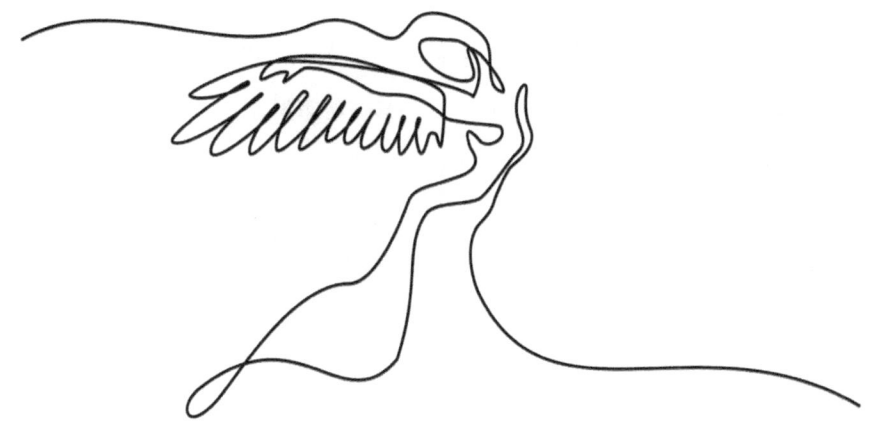

Chapter Eleven

The Archangels never did figure out how demons were getting into Theaa Academy. If they had, I'm not sure there would be anything I can do.

Marcus is the only surviving demon from the attacks that I can trust, and, even then, I'm not so sure. He's always been at least a little intimidating, and, on our first meeting, hurt me so bad that I thought he'd tear my wings out of my back..

"You want me to do what?" he demands at the lunch table later that day. I shush him, and he leans back and crosses his arms. A few people are looking at him, mostly girls that seem attracted to him. He stares them down until they look away giggling.

"I need you to get me back into Heaven," I say with a hushed tone. If we're overheard, the other students will probably just think we're weird, but I can't risk anything, not when we're so close to figuring all this out.

He grimaces and looks at the ceiling, thinking.

"I can get you promoted," I say. It's a risky move, but I think Lilith will accept it. She said I had to do anything it takes to rescue Desireé, and allying with Marcus must be included. How nice would it be for him to not just be a part of the lowly hoard of demonic soldiers?

He groans and slaps his hands down on the table.

"Fine. Fine. But you have to talk to Lilith first. If you die, I don't want to be screwed over."

Nadia rolls her eyes at him. She's sitting next to me today. After last night, we're uneasy friends, and Marcus had given her a disdainful look when we arrived in the cafeteria together. He can hate me all he wants. I just want to see Desireé again, and he's the easiest path to achieving that. "Deal," I say, holding my hand out. When he shakes it, he practically crushes my fingers, and I respond in kind with a terse smile.

"I hope you die," he says pleasantly.

"Likewise," I respond, mostly just to be as much of an asshole as him. I don't totally hate him, but I won't trust him for even a second.

I put my Hell phone in my backpack and call Lilith, the screen blocked from the rest of the student body seeing it.

"Avery. Have you finally come up with a plan?" she asks.

I frown. "Yes. But first, you need to promote Marcus. The plan sort of depends on him."

Lilith sighs, then nods. "Alright. It's done. Best of luck." I'm about to end the call when she says, "And remember, if you fail, there will be a war that kills millions on both sides. Maybe even billions."

Great. No pressure or anything.

I smile. "Thanks. I'll make sure to remember that. I almost forgot." Then, I hang up on her.

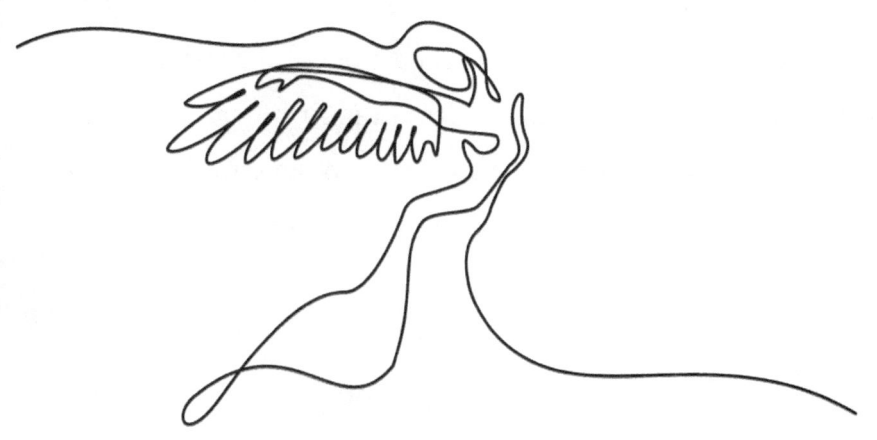

Chapter Twelve

It takes a week to prepare for the jump, mostly because I have to learn to transport myself from place to place so that I don't have to depend on the demons to do it for me. If an angel were to do it, I'd be sensed immediately and captured.

Gabe, the oldest student I'm friends with, appears in my room every night and runs through the spells with me so I can learn to teleport through space and time. The longer we practice, the further he sends me. At first, it's just from one end of my bedroom to the other.

The last practice jump I make before we set our

plan in motion lands me in Scotland, in the bedroom of a castle. There's a young woman inside,
asleep in her bed. The room is lit by candles, and
she's wearing something that looks straight out of
a movie. It's the year 1561, and that girl is Mary,
Queen of Scotts.

Holy shit.

I let out a giddy laugh, and Mary stirs. Before
she can spot me, I whisper the spell and appear
back in my bedroom.

"Well?" Gabe asks, leaning against the window-
sill.

I grin. "That was awesome."

He nods. "Well, I think you're ready. Good luck.
I hope I see you soon."

I wrap my arms around myself and nod.
"Thanks, Gabe." Gabe had been the first friend I
met when I arrived at Theaa Academy. If the plan
succeeds, I'll never get to see him again.

He wraps me in a reassuring hug, and I return
it with a sigh.

"I hope it works," I mumble into his shirt. He
pulls away, the ghost of a smile on his lips.

"It will," he says. He sounds so sure of it that I don't question him.

It has to work. We have one shot at this. If I fail, then the fate of the universe is at stake.

As soon as Gabe disappears, I take one final look around my room, taking it all in. I hated this place growing up, and I hated living with my dad. Now that he's trying, though, I'm sad to go.

I scrawl a note on a sheet of paper and place it on the the fridge under a magnet, along with a gift I got him during one of my lower-end practices earlier in the week. He should notice it as soon as he gets out of bed.

If I survive, I'll come back home to visit. He'll get better. If I don't, though, I want him to be okay.

I whisper the words that will take me away from here and leave this rickety home, probably for the last time.

Dad,

I'm going to be okay.

I bought two lottery tickets before I left. This one is for you.

Love,
Avery

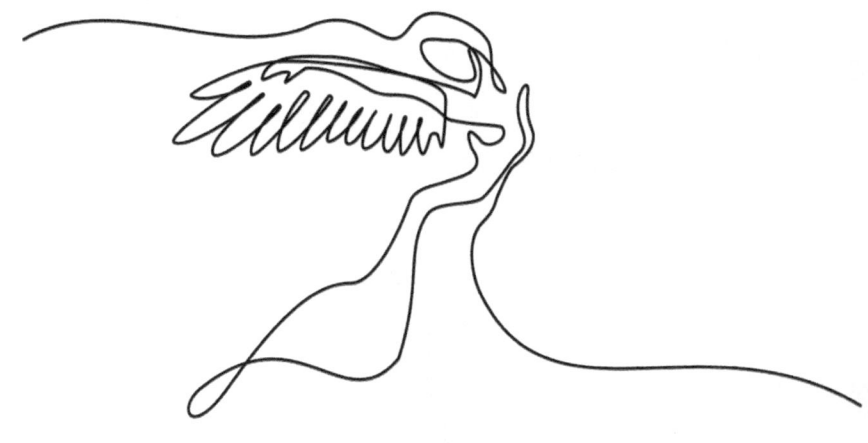

Chapter Thirteen

There's a portal to Heaven on Mount Everest.

In one of my classes when I was in high school, long before my death, I watched a documentary about Mount Everest. Some of the people who'd climbed the foreboding mountain had described impossible things. People joining them for their climbs and then disappearing. Hallucinations of people trying to lead them off sharp drops.

Now, though, I know the truth.

They hadn't been illusions.

They'd been demons, traveling through time to access this portal for the attacks I'd witnessed at

Theaa Academy.

I'm tempted to wrap my arms around myself. After all, how could I possibly survive these impossible conditions in leggings and a sweater? The frigid air doesn't bother me, though, and Marcus and Nadia don't seem put-out, either.

"About time," Marcus shouts over the howling of the wind. I roll my eyes and follow him, my sneakers plummeting into the snow. I consider whether it's reasonable to lodge a complaint with the Creator over her placement of mystical portals or not. My body may not be affected, but my clothes aren't doing too well.

There's a lot of space around the portal that isn't accessible by teleportation, which is how the demons found it in the first place. Desireé, the first to discover it, found it odd that nobody in all accounts of teleportation across Earth could enter this mile-wide dome. They always landed around it.

I know she'd spent a lot of time in Hell, but I don't want to know how long that must have been to read thousands of books on such a specific subject.

We have to hike to the dome, which is around the area known as Hillary's Step. It's a steep climb for those attempting to reach the peak, and we had to travel a decade back to ensure we arrived when it's still in-tact.

I keep my eyes ahead of us, ignoring the long-dead body in the snow as we approach the portal. If I look too close, think about it too hard, I might just be sick. Bodies are never recovered from Everest, and I can't be picky about the location of our transportation. There's nowhere else to enter Theaa Academy unseen.

As we approach, a flickering white in my peripheral vision catches my eye. A big gust of snow, perhaps? I glance over my shoulder. No. My wings. They're barely visible, but they're there. I let out a sigh of relief. It's almost like I've been holding my breath since I arrived back on Earth, and now I can breathe again. Marcus and Nadia's features are a little more drawn, a little sharper and less natural. When we exit Earth, we'll all look different.

Marcus places his bare hand on the stone, something that would give a human frostbite pretty much instantly, but doesn't affect him in the slightest. Within seconds, he disappears, although there's a sort of crackling energy against that side of the boulder now. Nadia takes my hand. She doesn't say it, but it's clear from her shaking that she's as scared as I am.

We walk through together, and I whisper one last "Goodbye" to Earth. Just in case I never make it back.

It's just like walking through a regular doorway. Nothing seems to happen, but we walk through and come out on a ledge at the face of a steep mountain. I can't see more than a dozen feet above or below us due to the thick cloud cover. I expect the ground to shake, but nothing happens. The wind from Everest is gone, leaving us in an eerie sort of silence.

"Why was there always an explosion before?" I ask. There's nobody around to hear us, yet I whisper.

"That only happens when we close the portal," Marcus says. "But Lilith said we need to be stealthy. In and out. We're going to keep the door open."

I frown. "But won't that mean anyone can go through?"

He waves me off but doesn't respond.

Okay, then.

I take in a deep breath.

I'm finally back in Heaven.

If the Archangels find out, though, then I'm sure to die.

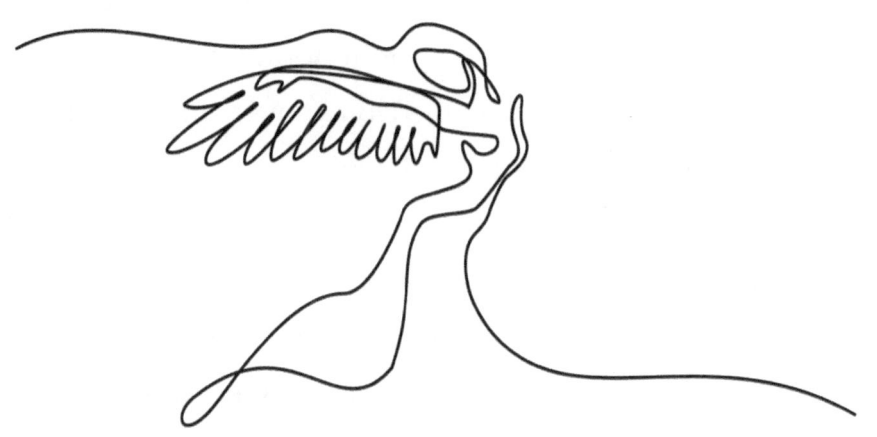

Chapter Fourteen

We have to scale the mountain to avoid being seen. Shockingly, I am not completely terrible at this, although it does take some getting used-to. Instead of pulling myself up with my arms, I learn fairly quickly that I have to push myself upward with my legs. The climb is tedious, but safer than flying in.

I tuck my wings against my back so they don't knock me off balance. I can catch myself if I fall, but I don't want that to be necessary, lest my wings become like a beacon to those on watch. On the bright side, Gabe had assured me that he would be one of the lookouts when we arrive, so we should be at least somewhat safe from prying eyes.

Finally, we get past the cloud cover, and Theaa Academy gleams a pearl white in the glowing night around us. Tears spring to my eyes immediately, and my heart aches. More than anywhere else in my life, this place felt like home. Now, though, I'm a fugitive. Hiding from those that I planned on spending an eternity with.

That's impossible now.

As we hop the barrier, onto a bridge that connects the hospital wing from the rest of the academy, a hand claps on my shoulder I nearly scream, but Gabe spins me around and shushes me. My heart is thumping so hard that I half expect it to break my ribs.

"We have to go," he says, grabbing my hand and dragging me through the halls. Nadia and Marcus follow us, and Gabe weaves us through the halls and into the belly of the school. I don't recognize the route, but when we come out in the small prison carved deep in the mountain, I gasp.

She's been here all along. It would have been so

easy for her to go with me when Nicolai sent me back to Earth the first time, but it hadn't happened. We'd all assumed that she'd been sent to the demon prison that the Archangels have on Earth, not kept in the same prison where I was held after my betrayal.

There are dozens of doors, almost exactly like the ones upstairs that lead to the student dorms. Huỳnh is down here waiting for us, and I run up and wrap my arms around her.

"There's no time," she whispers, and I pull away, wiping the tears off my cheeks. I nod.

"I can't figure out how to get to her," Gabe admits, hanging his head. "I know she's here, but these doors work differently than the ones upstairs."

I tilt my head, and my now white hair cascades down my shoulder. "How did you guys get me out?"

Huỳnh frowns. "We just said your name. But hers doesn't work when we try it."

I bite my lip. I have to think. Why would that work for me, but not Desireé?

When a door bangs upstairs, we all snap our heads up.

"We have to hurry," Huỳnh says urgently. If we're caught down here, we'll all be killed. Especially with the two demons that are standing guard at the entryway, their dark wings, horns, and ink-dipped hands standing in start contrast to the rest of the academy.

I rush over to one of the unmarked doors.

This had better work.

"Avery," I whisper. When she'd been in Hell, the name Desireé held onto had been mine, not hers. Maybe the doors don't go by someone's real name, but the name they respond to best.

With a click, the door opens. I'm about to go in, but something attacks me from behind.

"Die, bitch," Marcus hisses.

What the fuck?

I thought he was here to help me? Isn't that the order from Lilith?

Then I remember some of the things he's said to me. That he wishes I'd die. That he wanted me to secure his promotion if I didn't survive the mission.

The note on my locker. On my car. Those hadn't been a student that was mad about Desireé's death. They'd been *Marcus*.

And he's trying to tear out my wings again. His claws dig down beneath my skin, his talons scraping against the bone. I scream as the pain burrows deep into me, somewhere I don't think will ever go away.

I collapse to the ground. I can't even think well enough to summon my sword, and he's moving too fast. The attack has only been going on for a couple seconds.

Then, a form barrels out of the cell, a girl with leathery wings, spiral horns, and a pale face I know better than my own, dotted with freckles that look like dried blood with her pale demonic complexion.

She rips Marcus off of me, and I scuttle away, pulling myself up to a standing position just in time to see her slamming him to the ground.

"I've never liked you, Marcus," she says nonchalantly. Then, almost like it's happening in slow motion, she buries her own claws in his chest.

Deep.

Too deep.

My stomach wrenches.

She pulls out something I can hardly identify. It takes me a moment to realize what's happening.

His heart. She tore out his *heart*. She's done it so quickly that, for just an instant, Marcus stares at her with abject horror smattered across his face, which is covered in both red and gold blood.

Ruthless, he'd called her.

And now I know why. He hadn't even had the chance to fight back. And now he's dead. Sent to purgatory. His body fades into nothing, but his dripping heart remains in her grip.

Oh, god.

It shouldn't be possible for an angel, but I turn and vomit on the floor.

She looks at me, and her eyebrows scrunch together in concern. As soon as she's not looking at it, the heart fades to dust just like the rest of Marcus had. She rushes over to me and reaches forward, and I recoil. The hurt on her face makes me regret it instantly, but it's not like I can take it back.

"I'm sorry," I whisper, but she turns away.

"Um, guys?" Nadia says, her voice a squeak.

That's when the sound finally absorbs past everything else into my mind. Footsteps thundering down toward us.

The Archangels are coming.

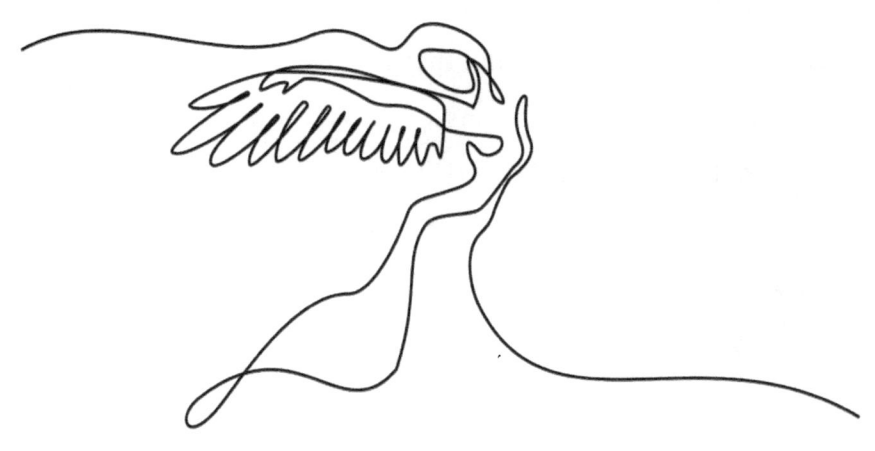

Chapter Fifteen

"You have to go," I hiss to my friends. Without protest or hesitation, Gabe and Huỳnh disappear in front of my eyes. Nadia whispers a spell and disappears as well, and a boom shakes the grounds. We hadn't told Marcus, but Lilith had ordered Nadia to destroy the Everest gate as soon as we escaped. There can be no more demons entering Theaa Academy. Desireé and I officially have no way out, not a way that can't be traced, anyway.

Desireé laces her fingers through mine, and I do my best to avoid flinching as I imagine the slick demon blood coating my palm. "You have to go," I say. If she goes, she can teleport back to Hell before the Archangels catch her. That is, as long as I can distract them for long enough.

She shakes her head. "No. We're doing this together."

I set my jaw and stare into her eyes, waiting to see who wavers first.

Neither of us does.

Despite the gruesome display, our relationship is going to be fine. She may be a ruthless killer, but she's mine.

The first to round the corner is Gabriel, who is very clearly pissed. I squeeze Desireé's hand and let go, raising my hands in the air, a symbol of surrender. Maybe, just maybe, we can avoid being killed.

Azrael comes next, although she doesn't seem nearly as shocked to see us as I'm expecting.

"Avery," she says, not a question, but an acknowledgement. She's been expecting me to show up.

"Azrael," I say, nodding once. Then, I do the same for Gabriel. I want to hide my fear as much as possible. No matter what happens, I will not be weak as they decide what to do with me. For Desireé, I have to be strong.

Before I can do much else, Azrael whispers a spell, and a burning black metal wraps around my wrists, and I cry out. A matching gold chain appears on Desireé, but she doesn't respond at all. Not even a tick in her jaw.

"You will be tried for your crimes," Azrael says, her words stiff and emotionless. She'd been like a mother to me for so long that her disinterest is like a knife through my heart.

This time, we're put in a cell together, Gabriel leading us in by the chains. We don't resist, and he's not rough with us. Then, Azrael locks us in and begins to whisper a serie of spells. I gasp as the air seems to be sucked out of the room. The more spells Azrael lays on it, the worse I feel. I fall to my knees, and Desireé leans over me and rests her bound hands on my back.

"It's okay," she lies, stroking my back as best as she can. We're going to die. There's no two ways about it. I don't say that out loud, though. She knows it just as well as I do.

"I'm so sorry," I say, still gasping for air that isn't here. I don't need to breathe, not even a little, but one breath of oxygen might quell the panic bubbling over.

She sits and pulls me into her lap, and I let her. As I lean my head against her chest, I can't help but picture Marcus's still-beating heart in her hand.

There's no point in worrying about it. We're going to be destroyed and sent to purgatory, anyway.

"What's purgatory like?" I ask. I should've done some semblance of research on it when I had access to Theaa's immense magical library, but I hadn't cared to do so. It had seemed so unlikely that I would end up there.

Now, though, the not knowing is the worst part.

"Bad," Desireé admits. "Lilith once told me it was just an endless nothing. A place where souls go and are lost an alone for eternity."

I nod. That doesn't sound too terrible, but then I start to really think about it. Wandering an endless, lonely void forever, nobody to speak to, nothing to do. From what I've seen, even Hellish demons get some sort of recreational time. Or, at least, time where they're not being tortured or tormenting humans. To make her feel better, though, I say, "I think we can handle it." Not together, though. This is our last chance to be together. Who knows how long we have until the Archangels return and send us to our doom?

I tilt my head up and put my hands around Desireé's neck, using the chain to pull her face toward me and press my lips desperately to hers. If this is our last chance together, then I am going to take advantage of every moment we have. She hesitates, then kisses me back with a ferocity I've never known.

We kiss for what could be seconds but feels like hours, clinging to each other for our lives. There's nothing else we can do. We've exhausted all our options. There are so many spells on our cell that an army couldn't help us at this point, let alone my three friends.

I wish I could apologize for putting them in danger, but that's obviously never going to happen. So, for the time being, I just don't think about it. Thinking is pointless. I'll have an eternity to just think about things. For now, I need to *feel*.

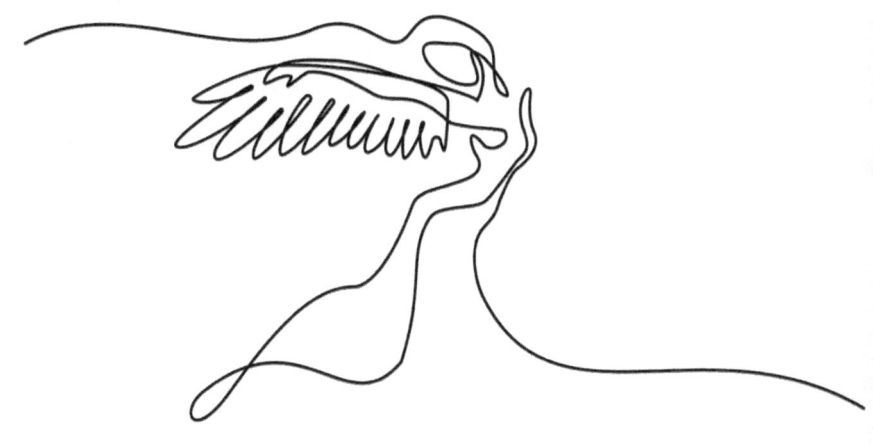

Chapter Sixteen

It's a long time before anyone comes to get us, days maybe, but it's not nearly long enough. I grip Desireé's hand in mine, holding on as tight as I can. When the door opens, a short, portly woman with straight black hair, dark skin, and a kind smile is standing there.

"Hello, darlings," she says, her voice upbeat. "I'm Michael. I'm here to take you to your trial."

This is absolutely not what I was expecting the most famous Archangel to look like, but I don't question it. Not when she could kill us at any moment. She doesn't comment on our tangled fingers and state of disarray, and we follow her up through the dungeons and out.

While the dungeon hadn't been dark, per-se, the light when we get upstairs is blinding. I gasp at the fresh air, sucking it all in like I've been suffocating.

We walk through the open-air walkways. We could just fly away, but Michael is the most dangerous creature in the entire universe, other than the Creator, of course. We can't risk it, not when there's the tiniest chance that we won't be slaughtered.

Unsurprisingly, we're led to the hospital wing, the first place I ever saw after my death. This is where Azrael explained that I was an angel, where I was sent when Desireé was first caught in my room. I half expect there to be a whole trial room set up, like something out of a movie, but there's not. It's just a small gathering of people, some of which have their backs turned.

Cain, though, is staring right at me. I would recognize Death anywhere, and my eyes lock on hers. Her expression is impossible to read, but I can't look away.

Azrael and Gabriel are here as well, and I can't place the final person.

When he turns around and extends his wings, it's like all the air is sucked from the room all over again. He's the most beautiful being I've ever seen, with skin as dark as the night sky and wings to match. His face looks like it was chiseled by the Creator herself, and tears prick at my eyes and my knees go weak. Looking at him feels a lot like heartbreak.

"Lucifer, how nice to see you again!" Michael says cheerfully.

Yeah, we're definitely going to die if the devil himself is here, consorting with angels. I tear my eyes away from his face. I may die today, but it absolutely will not be from looking at the devil.

"Michael," he says, his voice husky and tired, "I'd like to go ahead and get started, if that's alright with everyone else."

The Archangels mumble their agreement, and Azrael says, "You may both take a knee."

I stumble down to my knees, the position humiliating yet helpful. At this height, it's so much easier to avoid looking directly at Lucifer. Instead, I stare at his shoes, which are a plain pair of black Doc Martins.

Throughout all of this, Desireé's hand hasn't left mine. She squeezes, and I squeeze back.

"I love you," she breathes, and my heart beats just a little harder.

"I love you, too," I reply.

There's a ninety-nine percent chance that we'll be dead in five minutes.

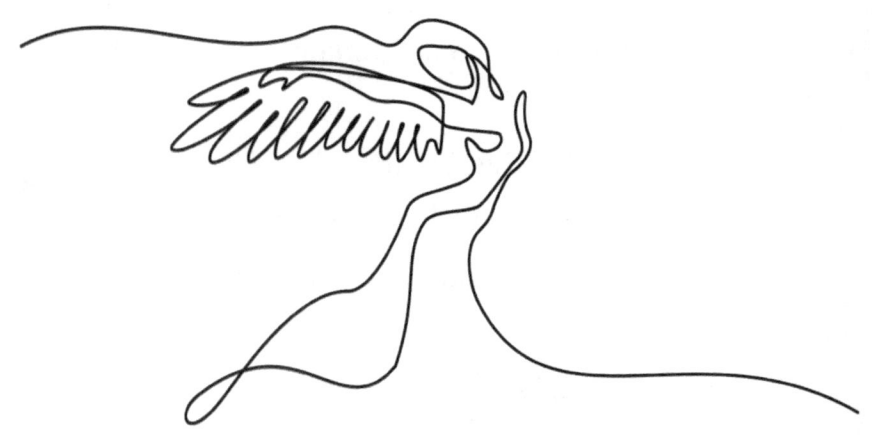

Chapter Seventeen

We are not given the chance to defend ourselves. Instead, Gabriel lists our crimes from one of those crystal phones, scrolling through them. I expect him to be pleased with himself. He's always seemed to hate me, but he just seems grim.

"Invasion of Theaa Academy, consorting with Angels, abandonment of post, murder of a fellow demon," he says, reading off everything Desireé has done. It's an absurdly long list, and several sets of eyes burn holes in my face. Still, I don't make eye contact with any of them. He keeps reading things, things I didn't know about. Apparently she gets into a lot of fights in Hell.

Azrael goes next, reading a list from her own device. These are my crimes, although the list is much shorter. "Consorting with a demon, treason, evading arrest, reckless endangerment of fellow angels," she says. The list doesn't go on like Desireé's had, though. I swallow. What if they kill Desireé in front of me and then just sentence me to imprisonment? Or torture in Hell?

When she's done with the list, the Archangels, Cain, and Lucifer all talk amongst themselves. I strain to hear their words, but they're so quiet that I can't understand them.

"What are they saying?" I mumble.

Desireé just shrugs, and her hand tightens on mine. My knees are getting sore from kneeling on the marble floor. It's not something I should be thinking about, but when I notice it, it's all that I can think about.

We sit there for hours while our jurors deliberate between themselves, discussing our crimes.

As the light outside begins to turn gold, Cain speaks up. "Alright," she says, "It is time."

Time for what? Our punishment?

She clears her throat, then walks toward us. When she stops mere steps away, I look up and into the depths of her eternal eyes.

"I will be speaking with the Creator to determine your guilt. If you are found guilty, Azrael will determine your punishment."

I nod the tiniest bit, and this seems to satisfy her.

Her eyes go from intense to blank in an instant. Is she able to communicate directly with the Creator? Is anyone else able to do that? What's the Creator like? I have a million questions racing through my mind, and I will never have the chance to ask them. I'll be too busy dying.

"Am I still needed?" Lucifer asks, clearly bored.

"No," Azrael says, disdain clear in her tone. It makes sense that they wouldn't like each other very much. He disappears, and the weight in the room becomes about a million times lighter than before.

We all wait for Cain, who stands stone-still. What's happening in her head? What is the Creator saying to her?

When the sky outside finally changes to hues of blue and purple, filled with more stars than should logically exist, Cain moves. It's just the slightest shift of her feet, but it's there. It takes her a moment to get her bearings, then she turns away from Desireé and I.

"Guilty," she says.

This whole time, I've thought that something, *anything*, might happen. That we'd be saved. But there's nobody coming. Nothing is going to stop Azrael from punishing us. This is the end.

"Before you punish us," Desireé says, surprising me, "Can I have one last moment with Avery?"

I look from Desireé's demonic yet beautiful face to the Archangels. Azrael frowns.

"I don't think that's necessary."

She's going to kill us, and it doesn't even matter to her. We're no more than nuisances. I should have known that, as soon as I betrayed the angels by showing my love for a demon, they wouldn't care about me anymore. I catch the tiniest flicker of what might be amusement in Gabriel's stare, but it's too quick for me to be sure. Of course he's going to enjoy this.

I'm weirdly calm, though. Whatever happens know, I know, at the very least, that I did every-thing I could.

"Alright," I say, swallowing down every emo-tion trying to escape and clamping them down. I will not cry. I will not beg.

It's time to die.

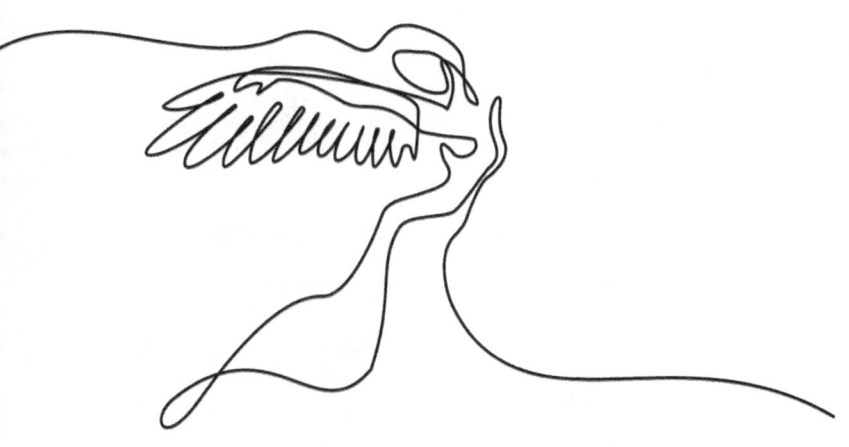

Chapter Eighteen

A zrael sighs and looks at her crystal Heaven phone, reading a statement like she's been practicing it.

"For the crimes listed, the angel Avery and the demon known to Heaven as Desireé and to Hell as Avery shall be punished. They will both be stripped of their ranks and banished from Heaven and Hell for one thousand years. After such time has passed, they may be allowed to re-apply for entry into Heaven."

Wait, what?

The words don't make sense, jumbling themselves around and around in my head until I'm dizzy.

Banished? Is that a way of saying we're being sent to purgatory?

She said something about a thousand years, though. Why would we be in purgatory for a thousand years? What does it even mean to re-apply for entry into Heaven?

I open my mouth, but no words come out. Just a tiny sound of protest. My body has been wound so tightly that I just can't react. Tears leak out of my eyes, and Desireé breaks out into hysterical laughter.

I turn to her, and my eyes widen. She releases my hand and falls to the ground in a fit of giggles, tears streaming down her face.

What the hell is going on?

Gabriel rolls his eyes.

"See you in a millennium," he says, then disappears without another word.

"I don't understand," I finally reply, my voice broken.

Azrael frowns. "I thought it was fairly clear."

She walks toward us, and I flinch, but she places her hands on each of us. "Have a good millennium."

In an instant, everything goes black.

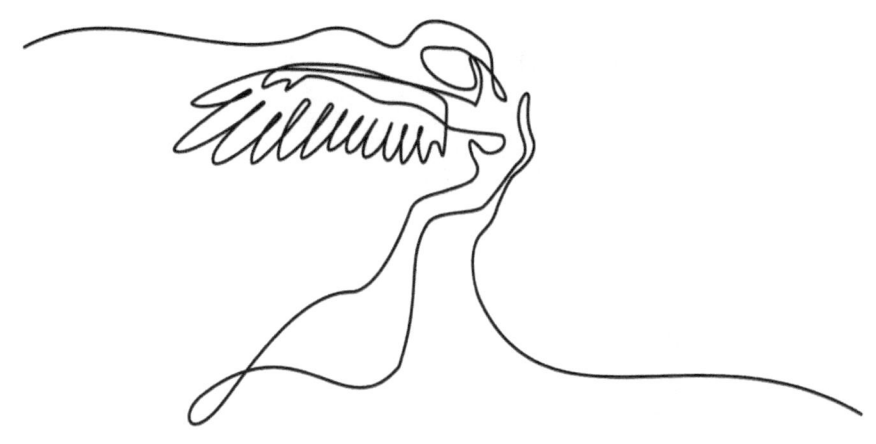

Chapter Nineteen

When I open my eyes again, I'm completely alone. I look around, and it's far too dark for me to see what's happening. Am I in purgatory? Has my thousand-year punishment begun? I suck in a breath, and the stale air chokes me.

I cough and hack at it, sitting up and leaning forward. I can't breathe here. My hands grasp at anything they can, and I find the roughness of my comforter.

Wait.

Am I on Earth?

Again?

I stand and stumble, and my eyes adjust slowly to the dark room. I flip the light switch on, absorbing my bedroom. This is wrong. It feels like I just woke up from a weird fever dream.

Then, something makes a jingling sound. It hasn't been long since I was here, but the phone's ringing startles me into action. I go back to my bed and pick it up, but the number isn't one that's programmed in. That's not too surprising, though, as this phone is new and only has five numbers in it. Anybody could be calling me.

I answer even though, based on the clock, it's four in the morning. "Hello?" I say carefully.

"Avery," the most perfect voice in the universe says with a sigh. It's not just anybody.

I close my eyes and let myself fall down onto my bed. "Desireé," I reply. It really is her. She's speaking to me.

"I remembered your number," she says. Then, after a pause and a male voice speaking in the background, she says, "Uh, can you come pick me up? I mean, I don't know if you have a car, since, you know…But maybe your dad's?"

I can't come up with the words. I'm going to see her again? For real? She will be in my arms? I would drive across the country and then sail across the ocean to get her. Compared to defying Heaven and Hell, it would be easy. When she clears her throat, I say, "Of course. Where are you?"

As soon as she gives me the name of the place, I run right to my car and start it up, tearing out of the driveway without a second thought.

There's a truck stop thirty minutes away, a dilapidated building with a gravel light and the permanent scent of cigarette smoke. My hands shake on the steering wheel, and I check the address on my phone once again. I hope she'd gotten it right. Then, a girl exits the building, silhouetted against the golden light inside. Still, I'd know her anywhere. Her gate is unsure as she approaches my car, so I leap out and run to her, gathering her in my arms, clinging to her for dear life.

"You're here," I say, breathing in her scent. She still smells a little sulfuric, but, mostly, she smells like she used to on Earth. She smells like home.

"So are you," she mumbles into my neck. I

laugh, and she responds in kind. This is all so unreal. Then, I remember what I did before I left.

"Want to go home?" I ask. "I left my dad a mysterious note, and I don't think he'd want to wake up to it."

She nods. "I'd like that. I'd like that a lot."

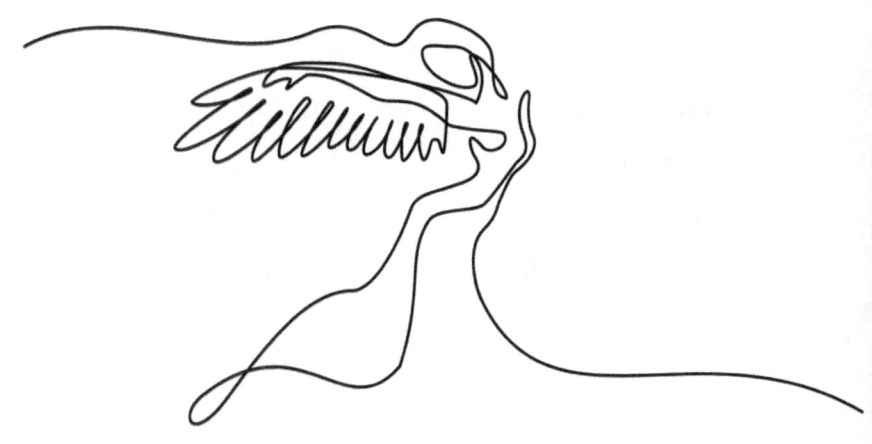

Chapter Twenty

We sneak back in the house, and I remove the note and lottery ticket from the fridge. I'll give the ticket to Dad when he's up. For now, I just want to stay by Desireé's side for as long as I can.

A thousand years. That's what Azrael had said. I have a thousand years on Earth with Desireé.

I recline on the couch instead of going to my room, and Desireé crawls into my lap, resting her head on my chest. Her hair is back to its human red color, and her skin no longer has that Hellish pallor. There's still magic coursing through me, though, so she must have the same.

"What are we gonna do for a thousand years?" she asks, her breath tickling my throat.

I tighten my arms around her and kiss the top of her head. "I don't know," I say honestly. I don't have anything to compare that sort of time to. Where Desireé had spent years and years in Hell, I'd only experienced one year in Heaven. What's it like for life to just keep on going for centuries?

"We could save the ocean," she suggests, and I laugh. It makes sense that her first thought would be to help others. That's just the kind of person she is.

"Or solve world hunger," I reply. In reality, the possibilities are endless. An angel and a demon with a thousand years to do anything we want? We could truly do everything.

And, with our ability to time travel, we could even make it last longer if we wanted to. We could help everybody. These aren't thoughts I would've had when I was alive, but I had done everything I could just to survive. Now that I have mystical powers, I don't have to worry about that. I can just focus on doing the things I want to do. With Desireé's enthusiasm for saving the world, I have a feeling that's what I'll want to do, too.

"I love you," I say, kissing her on top of her head once again.

"I love you too," she says.

"Forever?"

"Forever."

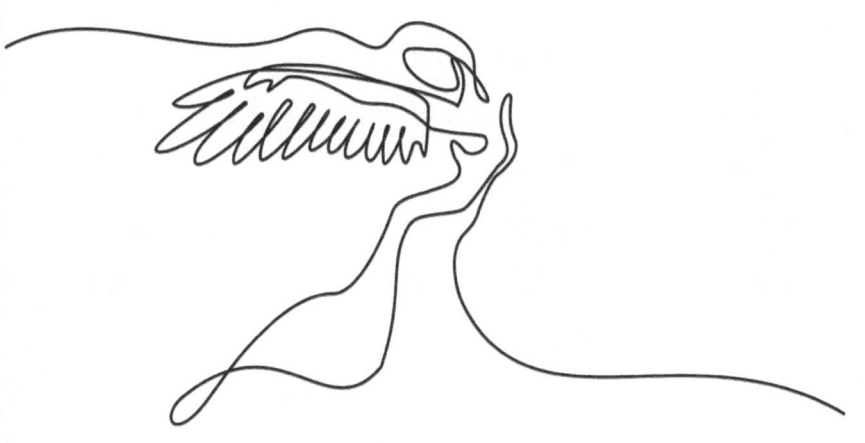

Chapter Twenty-One

Desireé's parents are ecstatic when they find out she's alive. Since her body hadn't been found, it had been easy to explain her disappearance as amnesia. She explains, honestly, that she doesn't remember how she got out of the car. Or much about her life. After she gets checked out by a doctor—Dr. Lilith Nassar—she's cleared to go back to her normal life.

We do all the normal stuff. We go to school. We attend prom. We go on dates. Dad buys a new house with the winning lottery ticket I'd given him, something modest and suburban. I encourage him to join us on weekends when we volunteer, and he seems to enjoy the work. After that, I convince him to go back to school so he can get a degree in social work.

College is long, but it's bearable when I spend it with Desireé. It helps, of course, that we can spend weekends teleporting to Paris or Hawaii or basically anywhere else we want. We start a company that recycles plastic from the ocean and sells it for a profit, which we then use to sponsor research into climate change. If we're going to be around for a thousand years, we need the planet to still exist by then. It's easier since Desireé can use her telepathic powers to prompt politicians into voting in the correct direction, at least.

She makes sure we age properly, although we still look like our ageless selves in private. We buy a small house in a small town, using our days to take care of a sprawling garden and every animal that wanders our way.

One day, when I'm reading a book in the garden pergola, Desireé approaches me and wraps her arms around me from behind.

"I was thinking about curing cancer this week," she says.

I tilt my head back and give her a small kiss. "That sounds great. I'll go ahead and get the research started twenty years ago, and you can gather funding."

She smiles. "Perfect."

Looking into her eyes, I realize that, yes, this is perfect.

And we still have nearly a thousand years left.

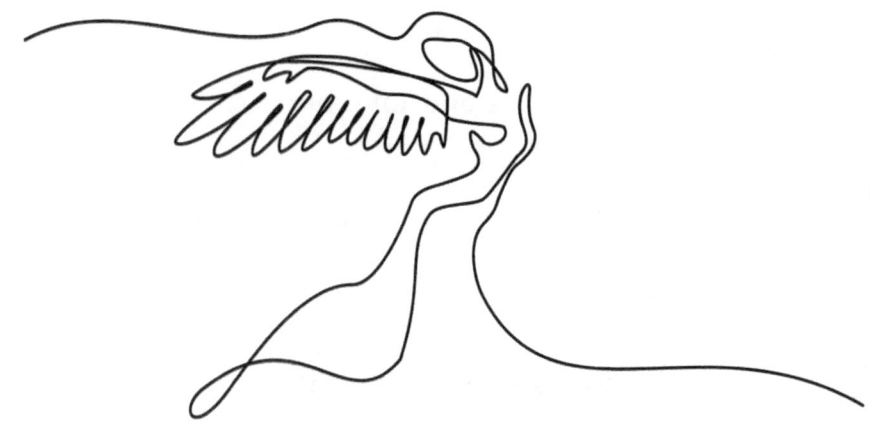

Chapter Twenty-Two

CASSANDRA

There's a cottage up the lane. It's small and ancient, but well tended. I grew up in this town my whole life, and I've spent plenty of time with the women who live there. Mom comments on how young they look for their age, although she never seems to sure as to what that age is, and Dad mumbles about me and my friends harassing them when we ride our bikes over.

"Don't be bothering that nice couple," he says. He's always worried about what people might think of him, and I roll my eyes.

They don't usually seem too bothered. They give us the freshest, fattest strawberries in the world from their garden, and they let Jimmy sit in the yard and play with their pack of dogs, who are all well-trained and polite. Better than my older sister's terrier that eats my shoes when I visit, at least.

"I won't," I promise, but I ride my bike up the lane anyway.

The blonde woman is waiting for me, smiling while she strokes a fluffy orange cat that basks in the patch of sun across her lap.

"Nice to see you again, Cass," she says. Her eyes wrinkle just a little at the corners when she grins.

"You too, Avery," I say. I take off my backpack and lift it. "I brought that book I told Desireé about."

Avery nods. "She'll like that. She's just at the store, but she'll be back soon." She stands and walks to the gate, opening it after commanding all the dogs to sit and wait. They always do, too.

"I have a question for you," I say slowly. It's not something I wanted to bring up, but everyone at school has been badgering me about it for basically forever.

She nods. "Go ahead."

"Well," I say, then bite my lip. What if she gets mad at me? Neither of them has ever gotten angry before, but they might, and that's what matters. Still, her face is open and friendly, so I continue, "Some people at school think you're witches. And that you're a thousand years old."

To my surprise, she laughs, tossing her head back.

"No, we're not witches. And we're not a thousand."

I nod. Right. I'm just being silly. Still, I have to ask. "How old are you then?"

This is a question Mom has told me never to ask people, especially the couple up the lane, but I don't care anymore. I have to know.

She scrunches her nose and leans forward, like she's letting me in on a secret.

"Promise not to tell anybody?"

I nod solemnly. If I were still thirteen, maybe I'd go around blabbing, but I'm going to be eighteen next month. I can handle this.

"We're turning a hundred sixty next year," she whispers.

My eyes widen. That can't be true, can it?

Still, I can't be certain. There have been strange things going on at this cottage my whole life. Animals that never seem to die, perfect plants, women who can be nowhere in sight one moment and standing right beside you the next.

I shouldn't believe her, but, for some reason, I do.

"Come on in," she says. "I had a feeling you'd be stopping by, and I made a cake."

The promise of cake distracts me just enough that I don't question her previous words.

Maybe I do live up the road from a couple of immortals, and maybe I don't. As long as she has cake, though, it doesn't really matter to me.

KATE HALL is a full time traveler, dog owner, artist, wife, and reader. She believes in wild things like love, magic, and basic human decency. Some of her least favorite things include selfish people, eating fish, and tornados. *Sign up for her mailing list for exclusive access to free short stories!*

www.KateHallBooks.com

Twitter @KateHallAuthor

Instagram @KateHallAuthor

Books By Kate Hall

From the world of ST. MERLIN'S ACADEMY:
Smoke and Mist
Ignite the Mountain

ANGEL ACADEMY
Angel Academy
Clandestine Angel
Renegade Angel

GINGER HILLS
The Girl in the Lake
The Girl Who Won't Drown
The Girls Down Below

VAMPIRE HUNTER CHRONICLES
Night Academy
Deadly Academy
Final Academy

SOUTHERN WITCHES
Southern Charms
Southern Spells
Southern Neromancy